dream Jobs ™

I want to be a
FASHION DESIGNER

PowerKiDS
press
New York

Mary R. Dunn

Dedicated to Ruth, my fashionable friend

Published in 2009 by The Rosen Publishing Group, Inc.
29 East 21st Street, New York, NY 10010

First Edition

Editor: Amelie von Zumbusch
Book Design: Ginny Chu
Layout Design: Julio Gil
Photo Researcher: Jessica Gerweck

Photo Credits: Cover, pp. 4, 8, 10, 14 (left), 14 (right), 18 © Getty Images; pp. 6, 12, 16, 20 © AFP/Getty Images.

Library of Congress Cataloging-in-Publication Data

Dunn, Mary R.
  I want to be a fashion designer / Mary R. Dunn. — 1st ed.
      p. cm. — (Dream jobs)
  Includes index.
  ISBN 978-1-4042-4472-6 (library binding)
  1. Fashion design—Vocational guidance—Juvenile literature. 2. Fashion designers—Juvenile literature.
I. Title.
  TT507.D86 2009
  746.9'2023—dc22

                                           2008000598

Manufactured in the United States of America

Contents

4

Kimora Lee Simmons is shown here with her daughters at a Baby Phat fashion show. Simmons designs the Baby Phat line.

What to Wear?

Are you one of those kids who loves to put together fun outfits and thinks a lot about what to wear? Do you like clothes and want to be in **style** and look great? Do you enjoy drawing and making things with your hands? Maybe you should think about becoming a fashion designer.

Fashion designers are artists who design, or plan, clothes and accessories, such as belts, handbags, and **jewelry**. Well-known fashion designers, like Kimora Lee Simmons and Isaac Mizrahi, get ideas from movies, art, and travel. They make clothing that people all over the world like to wear.

This model's dress was created by well-known Italian designer Valentino.

Fashion on Parade

One great place to see designer fashions is at a fashion show. There, people who love clothes can view **models** wearing the fashions in a designer's new **collection**. Models, such as Heidi Klum, can become famous, or well known, for wearing the beautiful clothes fashion designers **create**.

Awards shows are another big fashion **event**. The singers, actors, and other **celebrities** who are honored at these shows want to look their best. Movie stars, like Jennifer Hudson and George Clooney, wear designer clothes as they walk down the red **carpet** at events like the Academy Awards.

Celebrity Oprah Winfrey is shown here wearing a dress specially designed for her by Ralph Lauren (left).

Kinds of Fashion

Fashions worn by movie stars are often haute couture, or high fashion. Haute couture began in Paris hundreds of years ago. Designers dressed dolls in their new fashions. They sent the dolls to very rich **customers**, hoping these customers would order the one-of-a-kind designs. Today's couture designers make a small number of their creations and sell them in special stores.

Most people buy ready-to-wear fashions. These clothes are also created by a designer, but they are made in a factory and come in many sizes and colors. Ready-to-wear clothes are sold in lots of stores.

Models Carolyn Murphy (left) and Naomi Campbell (right) wore clothes designed by Anna Sui (center) at one of Sui's fashion shows.

Famous Designers

There are many famous fashion designers. For example, designer Anna Sui creates women's fashions and accessories, such as short dresses worn over turtleneck tops. Zac Posen makes fashions for men and women. He has designed several special styles of jeans.

Vera Wang, one of the top designers in the United States, grew up in New York. Wang became famous for her wedding dress designs. Actresses Jennifer Lopez and Uma Thurman wore wedding dresses created by Wang. At the Academy Awards, actresses Sharon Stone and Keira Knightley have walked the red carpet in Wang **originals**.

New designers learn how to sketch, or draw, fashions. They also learn how to pick fabrics to use in their designs.

Learning About Fashion

Many men and women who want to work in fashion go to design school. They take classes in art and learn about the rules of design, **pattern** making, **fabrics**, and sewing. As part of their training, they may also take computer classes that help with fashion creation.

People who want to design clothes also do on-the-job training. This means these designers work for a company. While working, they learn about fabrics and how to make clothing. At the same time, they find out how to market and sell new fashions.

Left: First Lady Laura Bush wore this gown designed by Oscar de la Renta. *Right:* Bush's dress was created from this drawing by the designer.

Thinking and Drawing

Designers want to create styles that many customers will like and want to buy. They study **trends** and come up with new ideas for clothes and accessories. Sometimes, designers read magazines or watch people on the street to get ideas. Designers also talk to buyers, or people who order things for stores.

After designers get an idea for a design, they make drawings of the garment, or piece of clothing. These drawings can be made by hand or with the computer. Young designers then generally take their designs to their boss for an approval, or okay.

Designers often put sample garments on dress forms, like this one, to show how the clothes would look on a person's body.

Cutting and Sewing

Once a design has been approved, designers pick the fabric with which to make the garment. Sometimes, they even design a new fabric pattern to use!

Next, the designers make a paper pattern of the garment. Some designers then make a copy of the garment out of a low-cost fabric called muslin. If the muslin garment looks good, a garment is made using the real fabric next. This new garment is called a sample. Designers use the cost of the fabric in the sample to help set the price for the piece of clothing.

Designers, like Vera Wang (right), often work with models behind the scenes at their fashion shows to make sure everything runs smoothly.

Fashion Shows

The sample garments in a designer's new collection may be shown at a fashion show. Fashion shows are busy events. Behind the scenes, models put on garments. People called stylists fix the models' hair and makeup. While the models get ready, buyers gather to see the parade of fashion.

When the show begins, models walk back and forth on a long runway. Designers often have between 50 and 100 garments in a season, so models need to change clothes often during the event. After the models have shown all the fashions, the designer walks the runway, too.

This Tommy Hilfiger fashion show was part of a group of fashion shows, called Fashion Week, in New York.

The Fashion Cities

Most fashion shows take place in Paris, Milan, London, or New York. Famous designers have fashion shows twice a year. During the summer, designers show their collections for the following fall and winter. They bring out spring and summer collections during the winter.

Each fashion city has shows by different designers. Paris holds shows by French fashion houses, such as Dior and Chanel. In Milan, design houses Versace and Prada are important. London is home to designers like Stella McCartney. New York, the fashion center of the United States, might show collections by Ralph Lauren and Donna Karan.

Getting into Fashion

If you want to become a fashion designer, you can prepare today. Take art classes, like drawing, painting, and design. Learn how to cut patterns and sew fabric, too. Carry a notepad and draw clothing designs you see. You can even make up designs of your own! Read about fashion in books and newspapers to learn about different designers. If you can, take part in community fashion shows.

If you work hard, you might become a top designer. You could mix with celebrities and walk the runway. Best of all, you could create beautiful clothes!

Glossary

awards (uh-WORDZ) Special honors given to people.

carpet (KAHR-pet) Rug.

celebrities (seh-LEH-breh-teez) Famous people.

collection (kuh-LEK-shun) A group of things.

create (kree-AYT) To produce or to make something.

customers (KUS-tuh-murz) People who buy goods or services.

event (ih-VENT) A thing that happens, often planned ahead of time.

fabrics (FA-briks) Cloths.

jewelry (JOO-ul-ree) Objects worn on the body that are made of special metals, such as gold and silver, and valued stones.

models (MAH-dulz) People whose job it is to show new clothes by wearing them.

originals (uh-RIJ-uh-nulz) Things that are one of a kind.

pattern (PA-turn) The way colors and shapes appear over and over again on something.

style (STYL) The look of something.

trends (TRENDZ) New ideas or styles.

Index

Web Sites

Due to the changing nature of Internet links, PowerKids Press has developed an online list of Web sites related to the subject of this book. This site is updated regularly. Please use this link to access the list:
www.powerkidslinks.com/djobs/fashion/

24